LIBRARY MOUSE
A World to Explore

DANIEL KIRK

SCHOLASTIC INC.
New York Toronto London Auckland
Sydney Mexico City New Delhi Hong Kong

Boone

For Ivy
—D. K.

ISBN 978-0-545-40463-1

12 11 10 9 8 7 6 5 4 3 2 1   11 12 13 14 15 16/0

Printed in the U.S.A.   40

First Scholastic printing, September 2011

The illustrations in this book were made with Winsor
and Newton gouache on Arches watercolor paper.
Book design by Chad W. Beckerman

SAM WAS A LIBRARY MOUSE. He lived in
a little hole in the wall behind the children's
reference books. Every night, he went looking
for adventure between the covers of books.

One evening, Sam went for a stroll. He smiled to see the class projects children had made to place atop the library shelves. A poster on the wall read, "Discover Our Great Big World."

"It *is* a great big world," Sam said, "and I love to read all about it."

Then he sighed, gazing at the books on the very top shelves, which were just a little too high for him to climb.

Suddenly, Sam saw something out of the corner of his eye. *Swoosh!* Another mouse landed gracefully on the floor right in front of him! "Whoa!" she said. "That was some ride. Good thing I had my parachute."

She stuck out her paw and smiled. "Hi, my name's Sarah. What's yours?"

"I—I'm Sam," he answered. "I live here!"

"I live here, too," Sarah said, "on the other side of the library. I was exploring, and that's when I discovered that playground!"

"Playground?" said Sam.

"Up high, on the shelves," Sarah explained, "you can almost see the whole world! I just went on that giant slide! I didn't know I was going to fall so far, though."

"You climbed all the way up there?" Sam asked. He had never dared to go all the way to the top.

"Sure," Sarah said. "I'm an explorer! All explorers climb."

Sam shook his head. "Well, that's not a slide. You just went down the side of a pyramid!"

"A what?"

"A pyramid," Sam said. "Like in ancient Egypt . . .
Only, children made this one. There are pictures of
real pyramids in these books you knocked off the
shelf."

"Wow!" Sarah said. "I didn't know there were
books about stuff like this!"

"Are there books about those other fun things I was climbing?" Sarah asked.

"You mean the Statue of Liberty and the Eiffel Tower?" Sam grinned. "Follow me!"

"We're going to do some research," Sam said. "We'll start with Egypt."

"What's research?" Sarah asked.

"It's how you find out about things," Sam said. "If you can't go to the real pyramids, you can read about them . . . right over here!"

Sam and Sarah pored over dozens of books, and Sarah oohed and aahed at the pictures. She gazed up at the tall shelves and said, "Research is fun. Let's climb up high and see what books are up there!"

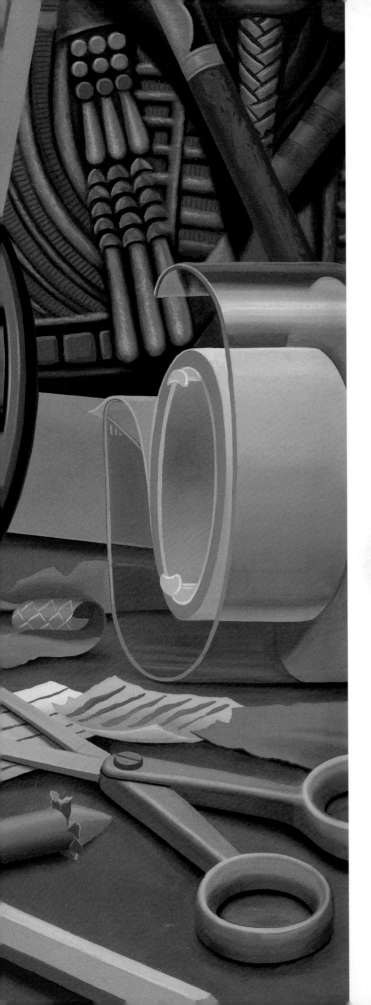

"Not tonight," Sam said,
looking warily at the tall shelves.
"Maybe we could play down here."
"Then let's pretend we're
pharaohs in ancient Egypt," Sarah
replied. "We can use these books
for research on how to dress up!"

It was nearly daylight when
Sam returned home. He picked
up his pencil to write about what
had happened. He had never met
anyone like Sarah before!

The next night, Sarah said, "There's a jeep up there that's just our size, Sam. Come on, we can pretend we're exploring and drive to the top of the tallest mountain!"

"I don't think you can drive to the top of the tallest mountain in a jeep," Sam said. "Besides, we can pretend from down here."

"You're not afraid, are you?" Sarah asked.

"Of course not," Sam said in a squeaky voice.

Sarah saw that Sam was nervous. "We could always do a little research first," she said.

"Good idea," said Sam.

While looking at a book about mountain climbers, Sarah had another idea. "I'll be right back," she said. She returned with some string and a paper clip.

"I'll hook one end of the string up at the top," she said. "Then I'll drop the other end down for you to tie around your waist. That way you won't have to worry about falling!"

"I'm not worried," Sam said as she started to climb. Soon it was his turn. He remembered he had read that when climbing he should not look down, so he didn't!

At the top of the shelf, Sam breathed a sigh of relief. It hadn't been as scary as he had thought it would be, and he and Sarah played and played until dawn.

Back on the ground, Sarah said, "You know, I'll bet we could explore even more of the world if we rode on that airplane over there!"

Sam looked up at the display the librarian had hung above the tallest shelves. "It doesn't really fly," he said, "and we couldn't reach it anyway!"

"I know it can't fly," Sarah said. "But think of how much of the world we could see from up there! We can climb to the top of this bookshelf, then jump over to the plane. It'll be easy!"

"But—"

Sarah wouldn't take no for an answer. "Sam," she said, "tonight we're going to get into that airplane, and we're going to see the world!"

Throughout the day, Sam was so nervous he could hardly sleep or read. He didn't want to let Sarah—or himself—down, but he didn't want to get into that airplane, either.

That night, Sarah led Sam to the top of the bookshelf. The airplane looked very far away.

"We're explorers, and good jumpers, too. We can do it!" Sarah said. Sam clenched his teeth and crept to the edge.

"Follow me," Sarah said, and then she jumped. Sam jumped, too, and climbed into the seat behind Sarah.

"We're off to see the world!" she cried. But just at that moment, the string that held up the airplane broke!

"Wooo-hoooo!" Sarah hollered.

"Aaaaaaaah!" Sam screamed.

They sailed over the Eiffel Tower and the Great Wall of China, over the Statue of Liberty and the Great Pyramids.

They sailed past volcanoes and mountaintops, past coral reefs and deserts, between dark rows of bookshelves, and right out the door of the children's room.

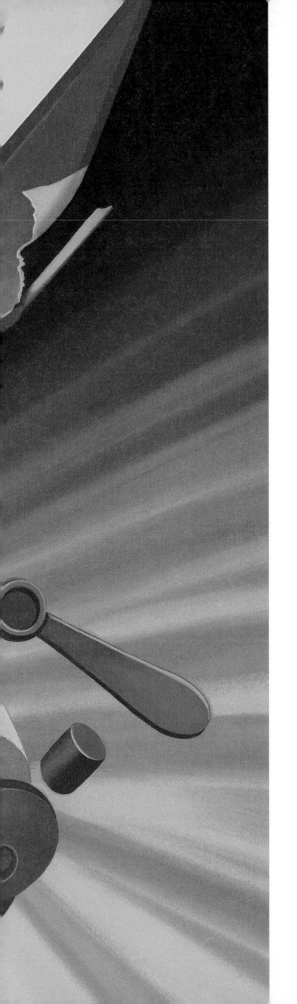

The airplane bumped to a stop in the dark hallway. Sam leaped out of his seat. He didn't stop running until he was back in his little hole in the wall.

"Sam!" Sarah cried. "Come back! Explorers don't run from danger!"

Sam hid behind his bed and wouldn't come out. But later, when his heart stopped pounding, he went to his writing desk, picked up his pencil, and got to work on a new project.

"Readers and writers are explorers, too," he said.

"Wow," Sarah said the next evening when she saw Sam's book, *Sam and Sarah See the World*. "We're both a couple of explorers!"

"And we never even had to leave the library!" said Sam.

"We didn't *have* to leave the library," Sarah said with a twinkle in her eye, "but just think of the books you could write if you really got to see the world! What do you say we take a little research trip?"

As they strolled through the library, Sam didn't know what to say. He had never met a mouse like Sarah!